This book belongs to:

....

....

Bright Sparks books have been created
with the help of experts in early childhood education.
They are designed to help young children achieve
success in their early learning years.

Retold by Sue Graves
Illustrated by Andrew Breakspeare

Reading consultants: Betty Root and Monica Hughes

This is a Parragon Publishing book
First published 2006

Parragon Publishing
Queen Street House
4 Queen Street
Bath BA1 1HE, UK

Copyright © Parragon Books Ltd 2006

ISBN 1-40547-966-3
Printed in China

Chicken Little

p

Helping your child read

Bright Sparks readers are closely linked to recognized learning strategies. Their vocabulary has been carefully selected from word lists recommended by educational experts.

Read the story

Read the story to your child a few times.

"Oh dear," said Foxy Loxy. "You are going the wrong way."
"Oh no!" said Chicken Little. "What shall we do?"
"Follow me!" said Foxy Loxy. "I will show you the way."

20

Follow your finger

Run your finger under the text as you read.
Soon your child will begin to follow the words with you.

6

Look at the pictures

Talk about the pictures. They will
help your child understand the story.

"Follow me!"

21

Give it a try

Let your child try
reading the large
type on each
right-hand page.
It repeats a line
from the story.

Join in

When your child is ready,
encourage him or her to join in with
the main story text. Shared reading
is the first step to reading alone.

Chicken Little was a little brown hen.
She lived on a farm with lots of other
animals.
Every day she sat under a big oak tree.
One day an acorn fell down.

An acorn fell down.

The acorn fell on
Chicken Little's head.
"Ouch!" said Chicken Little.
She looked up at the sky.
"The sky is falling!" she said. "I must
tell the king. He will know what to do."

"The sky is falling!"

On the way, she met Cocky Locky.
"Where are you going?" asked
Cocky Locky.
"I am going to see the king," said
Chicken Little. "The sky is falling!
He will know what to do."
"I will come with you," said
Cocky Locky.
So Chicken Little and Cocky Locky
ran on.

She met Cocky Locky.

On the way, they met Ducky Lucky.
"Where are you going?" asked
Ducky Lucky.
"We are going to see the king," said
Chicken Little. "The sky is falling.
He will know what to do."
"I'll come with you," said
Ducky Lucky.
So Chicken Little, Cocky Locky, and
Ducky Lucky ran on.

"We are going to see the king."

On the way, they met Goosey Loosey.
"Where are you going?" asked
Goosey Loosey.
"We are going to see the king," said
Chicken Little. "The sky is falling.
He will know what to do."
"I'll come with you," said
Goosey Loosey.
So Chicken Little, Cocky Locky, Ducky
Lucky, and Goosey Loosey
ran on.

"I'll come with you."

On the way,
they met Foxy Loxy.
"Where are you going?" asked
Foxy Loxy.
"We are going to see the king," said
Chicken Little. "The sky is falling.
He will know what to do."

On the way, they met
Foxy Loxy.

"Oh dear," said Foxy Loxy. "You are going the wrong way."

"Oh no!" said Chicken Little. "What shall we do?"

"Follow me!" said Foxy Loxy. "I will show you the way."

"Follow me!"

They went on and on until they came
to a cave.
"Follow me!" said Foxy Loxy.
Goosey Loosey, Ducky Lucky, Cocky
Locky, and Chicken Little followed
Foxy Loxy.
But it wasn't a cave.
It was Foxy Loxy's den.

It was Foxy Loxy's den.

Suddenly, Cocky Locky cried out,
"Cock-a-doodle-doo!"
"Oh no!" said Chicken Little. "I must
run away. I must run away!"
Chicken Little ran away from
Foxy Loxy's den.

"I must run away!"

Chicken Little ran all the way home.
She was a very lucky chicken.
And she never did tell the king that
the sky was falling.

Chicken Little ran home.

Look back in your book.

Can you read these words?

acorn

Chicken Little

Ducky Lucky

Cocky Locky

Foxy Loxy

Goosey Loosey

Can you answer these questions?

What fell on
Chicken Little?

Whom did Chicken
Little meet first?

Who said, "Follow me!"?

The End